little Miss Lucky

by Roger Hargreaves

WORLD INTERNATIONAL

MANCHESTER

Little Miss Lucky lived on top of a hill in Horseshoe Cottage.

One evening, after supper, she went to bed with a book she had bought that morning.

She loved to read, and the place she loved to read most was in bed.

Do you like reading in bed?

Lots of people do!

It was a cold and windy winter's night outside, but little Miss Lucky snuggled down under the blankets and was as warm and cosy as could be.

She opened the book and started to read the first page.

But as she did so, there was a knock on the front door of Horseshoe Cottage.

KNOCK! KNOCK! KNOCK!

"Oh bother," she thought to herself. "Who can that be at this time of night?"

KNOCK! KNOCK! KNOCK!

There it was again.

She put her book down, got out of bed, and went downstairs to see who was there.

Little Miss Lucky unlocked the door and opened it.

But there was nobody there!

She peered outside.

Nobody!

She went outside.

Nobody!

Then, suddenly, there was a huge gust of wind and the door banged behind her.

BANG!

She nearly jumped out of her skin.

She tried to open the door, but it had locked itself and she couldn't open it.

"Oh dear," she gasped. "What am I to do?"

I wonder why this story is called 'Little Miss Lucky'?

She ran around Horseshoe Cottage to see if she could get in through the back door, but as she did so there was an even bigger gust of wind.

A really huge, enormous, gigantic gust
of wind!

It was so strong that it lifted little Miss Lucky
off her feet and up, up into the air.

And up!

"Help!" she cried.

"Somebody help!"

But her little voice was lost in the whistling of the wind.

Higher and higher she was taken, up and up into the night.

But then, just as suddenly as it had started, the wind stopped.

And there was little Miss Lucky, high in the air! She started to fall.

Down and down.

I wonder why this story is called 'Little Miss Lucky'?

Faster and faster she fell towards the ground.

Oh!

She landed in a haystack in the corner of a field.

Little Miss Lucky gasped for breath, and felt to see if she had broken any bones.

But the haystack had cushioned her fall, and apart from feeling very frightened she was all right.

She climbed down from the haystack, and ran as fast as she could across the field looking for somebody to help her.

Looking for anybody to help her!

It was very dark, and little Miss Lucky could scarcely see where she was going.

There was a tree in the middle of the field, and little Miss Lucky tripped over one of its roots.

It was then that she heard the voice.

"HELLO," it said, "WHO HAVE WE HERE?"

Little Miss Lucky shivered.

"Who's there?" she whispered.

"I," chuckled the voice, "AM THE MIDNIGHT TREE!"

And, as little Miss Lucky looked at the tree, she saw that it had a face.

Not the sort of face you would like to see on a cold, dark, windy winter's night.

I wonder why this story is called 'Little Miss Lucky'?

The tree grinned, and reached out one of its branches.

Oh!

Little Miss Lucky jumped to her feet and ran away as fast as ever her legs could carry her.

As far away from that tree as possible.

But, as she ran, she heard a noise behind her.

THUD!

THUD!

THUD!

She looked over her shoulder, and couldn't believe her eyes.

THUD!

THUD!

THUD!

The tree was chasing her!

Oh!

She ran faster than ever!

THUD!

THUD!

THUD!

But the tree was getting closer!

THUD THUD THUD!

Little Miss Lucky stopped, and shut her eyes. Tight!

THUD!

I wonder why this story is called 'Little Miss Lucky'?

THUD!

Little Miss Lucky opened her eyes.

Wide!

The book she had been reading in bed had slipped from her fingers and fallen on to the bedroom floor.

THUD!

She had fallen asleep reading her book!
It had all been a dream!
A dream!
No knock at the door!
No terrible wind!
No Midnight Tree!
A dream!

And now you know why this story is called 'Little Miss Lucky'.

Don't you?

SPECIAL OFFERS FOR MR MEN AND LITTLE MISS READERS

In every Mr Men and Little Miss book you will find a special token.
Collect only six tokens and we will send you a super poster of your choice
featuring all your favourite Mr Men or Little Miss friends.

And for the first 4,000 readers we hear from, we will send you a
Mr Men activity pad* and a bookmark* as well – absolutely free!

Return this page with six tokens from Mr Men and/or Little Miss books to:
Marketing Department, World International Publishing, Egmont House,
PO Box 111, 61 Great Ducie Street, Manchester M60 3BL.

Your name: _____

Address: _____

_____

_____ Postcode: _____

Signature of parent or guardian: _____

I enclose **six** tokens – please send me a Mr Men poster ☐

I enclose **six** tokens – please send me a Little Miss poster ☐

We may occasionally wish to advise you of other children's books that
we publish. If you would rather we didn't, please tick this box ☐

*while stocks last   (Please note: this offer is limited to a maximum of two posters per household.)

Collect six of these tokens.
You will find one inside every
Mr Men and Little Miss book
which has this special offer.

1 TOKEN

Please remove this page carefully

MR MEN question time – can you help?

Thank you for purchasing this Mr Men or Little Miss pocket book. We would be most grateful if you would help us with the answers to a few questions.

Would you be interested in a presentation box
to keep your Mr Men or Little Miss books in?   **Yes** ☐ **No** ☐ (please tick)

Apart from Mr Men or Little Miss, who
is your favourite children's character? _____

If you could write a Mr Men and a Little Miss book,
what names would you give your characters?   **Mr** _____

                                                Little Miss _____

If applicable, where did you buy this book from?
Please give the stockist's name and address.

Name: _____

Address: _____

_____

_____

THANK YOU FOR YOUR HELP